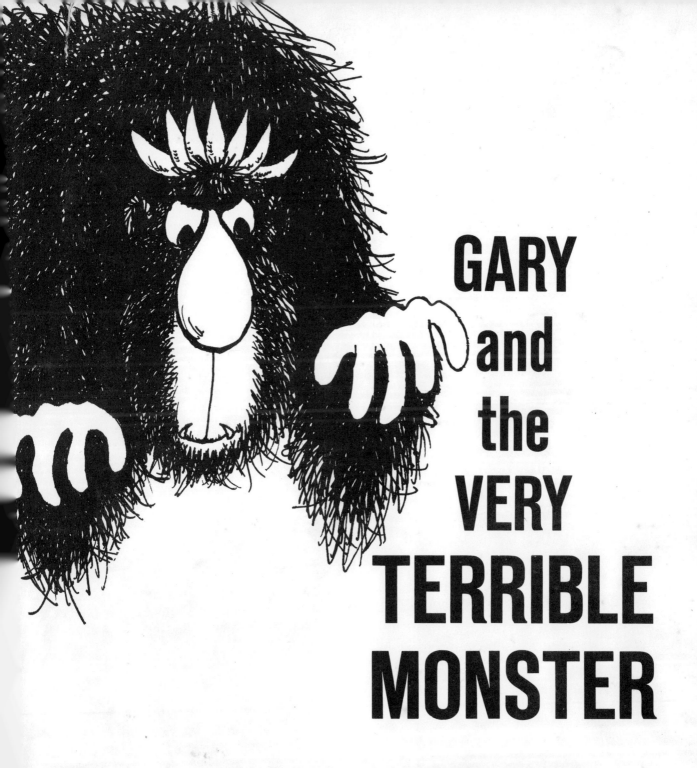

# GARY
## and
## the
## VERY
## TERRIBLE
## MONSTER

By Barbara Williams
Illustrated by Lois Axeman

CHILDRENS PRESS, CHICAGO

**Library of Congress Cataloging in Publication Data**

Williams, Barbara.
  Gary and the very terrible monster.

  SUMMARY: The trouble-causing monster that only
Gary can see disappears when he gets a real puppy.
  [1. Pets—Stories] I. Axeman, Lois, illus. II. Title.
PZ7.W65587Gar      [E]      72-8435

7 8 9 10 11 12 13 14 15 16 17 18 19 20 21 22 23 24 25 R 79 78 77 76

When Gary was five, he had a pet monster.
A very terrible monster.
His name was Mr. Green Nose.
He had a green nose
and long black hair
and red eyes
and seven yellow horns
and a tail that could throw rocks.

Mr. Green Nose could grow tall.
As TALL as a house.

Mr. Green Nose could grow small.
As small as a mouse.

He made a terrible noise. A very terrible
noise. A noise like a little boy burping.

Mr. Mudd lived next door. He could not see Mr. Green Nose. He did not know about monsters. They throw rocks. Mr. Mudd thought Gary threw the rock. It went through Mr. Mudd's window. It flew by his nose. It hit his goldfish bowl. Out went five gold fish and two black ones.

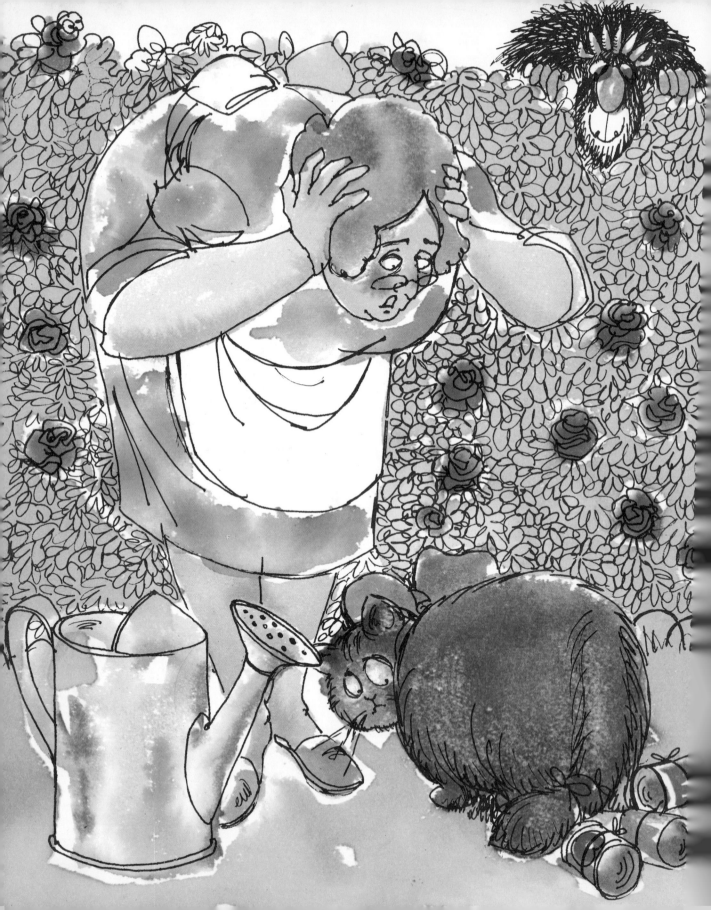

Miss Fitt lived down the street.
She could not see Mr. Green Nose.
She did not know about monsters. They
are bad to small animals. She thought
Gary put the cans on her fat cat.

The paper boy could not see Mr. Green Nose. He did not know about monsters. They like to build things. He thought that Gary left the nails in the street. The nails made holes in his bicycle tires.

Gary's teacher could not see Mr. Green
Nose. She did not know about monsters.
They don't like girls. She thought Gary
put the fly in Debbie White's milk. It made
Debbie cry.

No one else could see Mr. Green Nose. Only Gary.

Gary *told* people about Mr. Green Nose. He told his dad and mother. But dads and mothers are funny. They do not believe in monsters. Gary's dad and mother could not see Mr. Green Nose. They thought it was Gary who did all the bad things.

They thought Gary left his wagon
out in the rain.

and left skates on the stairs

16

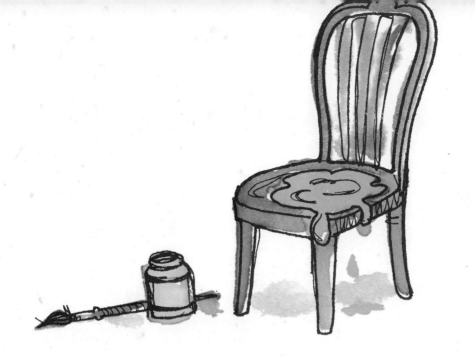

and got blue paint on the chair

and made those terrible burping noises.

Gary was sorry that Mr. Green Nose
was bad. But Gary could not get rid of
him. How do you get rid of a monster
with a green nose and long black hair
and red eyes
and seven yellow horns
and a tail that throws rocks?

One day Gary and his monster went
for a walk. They came to a pet store.
In the window was a brown puppy. It
looked at Gary with big eyes.

Gary went into the store. He asked the man if he could hold the puppy.

The man said yes. Gary took the puppy. Her tail went fast.

"What is her name?" asked Gary.

"Cookie," said the man. "She likes you. You may play with her. But we may sell her soon. She will make a good watchdog for some boy."

A watchdog? A WATCHDOG? Gary had an idea. He put Cookie down. He ran all the way home.

Gary told his mother about his idea. She was not sure it would work.

"Monsters are bad," she said. "They do not like small animals. Mr. Green Nose might put cans on Cookie. Or throw rocks at Cookie. Or put nails in Cookie's doghouse. Or put a fly in her bowl."

"Oh, no," said Gary. "Cookie is a WATCHDOG. Mr. Green Nose is afraid of Cookie."

"How do you know?" asked Gary's mother. "He was afraid in the pet store," said Gary. "He hid in my pocket. He did not burp once."

Gary's mother thought about it. She
talked to Gary's dad. They said they
would try it.

The next day Cookie came to Gary's
house. She came to live. She looked all
around. She yipped and yipped. She
scared Mr. Green Nose away. He never
came back.

Now no rocks fly through Mr. Mudd's window. Sometimes he asks Gary and Cookie into his house. He shows them his new fish bowl. It has six gold fish. And three black ones.

Now there are no nails in the street.
There are no holes in the paper boy's
tires. Sometimes Gary and Cookie help him.

Now there is no fly in Debbie White's milk. Gary brings Cookie to school for Show and Tell. Debbie plays with Cookie. Cookie makes Debbie laugh.

Now Gary's wagon comes in when it rains,
and no one leaves skates on the stairs
or gets paint on the chairs
or makes terrible burping noises.

Now there are no cans on Miss Fitt's fat
cat. But the cat does not like Cookie. She
climbs a big tree to get away. Miss Fitt
calls the firemen. They get the fat cat down.

The cat thinks Cookie is a monster. Miss Fitt thinks Cookie is a *terrible* monster. But everyone else is happy . . . most of all Cookie and Gary.

31

*About the Author:* Barbara Williams has been writing since she was old enough to hold a pencil and publishing since she was in grade school. In addition to *Gary and the Very Terrible Monster*, she has had twelve books, three plays, and a number of magazine stories, poems, and articles published. Her writing covers a wide range of interests—from childrens' picture books to college textbooks—but she is happiest when working on something whimsical. Mrs. Williams now lives in Salt Lake City with her husband and children. She loves to travel with her family, especially to places of historical interest.

*About the Artist:* Lois Axeman is a native Chicagoan who lives with her husband and two children in the city. After attending the American Academy and the Institute of Design (IIT), Lois started as a fashion illustrator in a department store. When the childrens wear illustrator became ill, Lois took her place and found she loved drawing children. She started free-lancing then, and has been doing text and picture books ever since.